The Angel
and the Soldier Boy

PETER COLLINGTON

Methuen Children's Books · London

For Bonnie and Sasha
Special thanks to Ross and John

First published in Great Britain in 1987
by Methuen Children's Books Ltd
First published in Great Britain in this miniature edition 1990
by Methuen Children's Books
Michelin House, 81 Fulham Road, London SW3 6RB
Copyright © Peter Collington 1987
Printed and bound in Hong Kong

CIP data for this book is available from the
British Library
ISBN 0 416 16662 8

The artwork is executed in
coloured pencil and water colour on card.

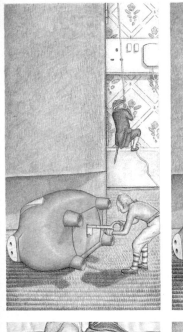

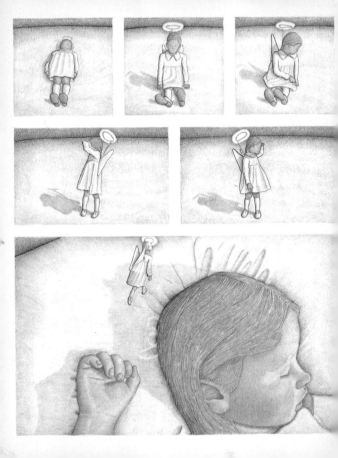

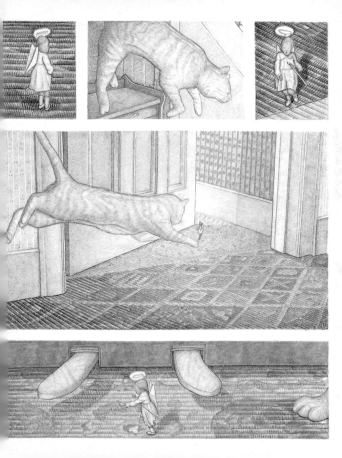

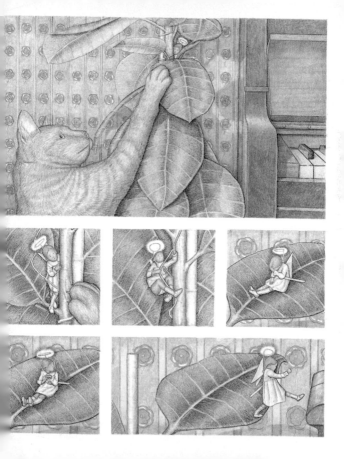

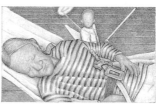

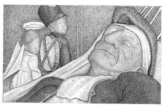

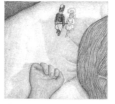